This edition published 1990 by Guild Publishing
by arrangement with Walker Books Ltd

Text © year of publication individual authors
Illustrations © year of publication individual illustrators
Cover and title page illustration © 1985 Helen Oxenbury
Illustrations pp 14-15 © 1990 Helen Craig
Illustrations pp 36-37 © 1990 Penny Dale

First printed 1990
Printed and bound in Hong Kong
by South China Printing Co. (1988) Ltd

CN 6243

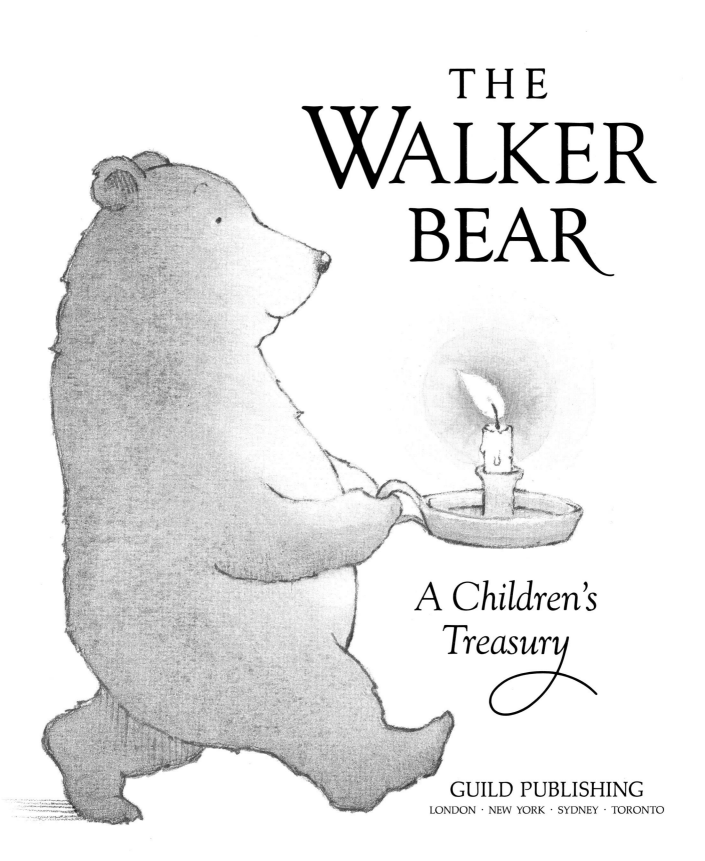

THE
WALKER
BEAR

*A Children's
Treasury*

GUILD PUBLISHING
LONDON · NEW YORK · SYDNEY · TORONTO

CONTENTS

This book is really 35 books or bits of books all wrapped in one. The original books come in many shapes and sizes. There are tall books and short books, fat books and thin books, books which are almost all pictures, books which are almost all words. But they all exist for the same reason, to give pleasure to children, and hopefully to the rest of the family as well.

You may have read some of the original books already, but if not they can be found in bookshops or libraries. One way to recognize them is by looking for the Walker Bear, whose picture is on the spine or title page or cover. But the best way is to know the name of the book, and who wrote it and who drew the pictures. All the original titles are given on pages 92-93, together with a list of other books by the same authors and illustrators.

Now these 35 books are gathered together in one place, as if they're at a party; and this book *is* a sort of celebration. For one thing it celebrates the skill and humour and high spirits of all the people who made it – the storytellers, in words and pictures. For another it is the first volume of *The Walker Bear*, and there's going to be a new volume every year. And last but not least (as the Walker Bear is not shy to point out), Walker Books has now been publishing children's books for ten years … so it's the Walker Bear's tenth birthday.

The Walker Bear welcomes you to the party and hopes you have a truly wonderful time.

Tom and Pippo Read a Story
by Helen Oxenbury

I like to look at books, but best of all I like to look at books with Daddy.

Daddy likes to look at his paper, but he doesn't mind reading my books to me.

When Daddy's finished reading
to me, I think Pippo would
like to hear a story.
So I bring Pippo and ask
Daddy to read to him.
When Daddy says he
really can't read any
more books, I read to Pippo.

I hope one day Pippo can read on his own.

They came from Aargh!

by Russell Hoban

illustrated by Colin McNaughton

They came from Aargh! They came from Ugh! They came from beyond the galaxy.

All of them were alien, all of them were strange. Their ship was strange and alien, it had twelve legs.

Their battle cry was, "Three chairs for Aargh! Three chairs for Ugh!"

Commander Blob read out the readout on the big display.

He read, "Zom! Zeem! Plovsnat! Ruk!"

Navigator Blurb was taking a star sight. "Ruk fifteen point vom," he said.

"Plovsnat at thirty-seven zeems and holding vummitch."

"Vummitch it is," said Commander Blob. "I'm taking her in."

Technician Bleep was on the scanner.

"What do you scan?" said Blob.

"Cay!" said Bleep. "Chah!"

"Chocolate cake," said Blub. "Prepare to land," said Blob.

"Four legs down," said Blub. "Eight legs down. Twelve legs down."

"Jets on full, jets on half, jets on quarter, we're down," said Blob. Ssssss! went the airlock, and out they came, moving slowly, moving carefully, looking all round slowly and carefully.

They had their bimblers ready, they had their globsters on as well, they had their cake beam going.

"Is there intelligent life on this planet?" said Blub.

"Nobody knows," said Blob.

"Keep your globster and your bimbler ready, we don't know what we might run into."

"Chah!" said Bleep.

Bzzzzzzzt! Bzzzzzzzt! went the cake beam.

"He's beaming us into the chocolate cake," said Blob.

"Look out," said Blub, "there's something coming."

"What is it?" said Blob.

"It's shocking and horrible," said Blub.

"It's a shock horror," said Blob.

"It has seven heads and five wings," said Blub.

"It's flying in a circle," said Blob.

"That's because it has three wings on one side and two on the other," said Blub.

"It's an asymmetrical shock horror," said Blob.

"We'd better bimble it before it bimbles us."

"Let's try giving it some milk," said Blub. "It may be friendly."

They gave the asymmetrical shock horror some milk. It purred as it lapped it up.

11

"Put that in your report," said Blob to Blub.

"Blub reporting to base," said Blub into his helmet radio. "Asymmetrical shock horror fond of milk, purrs."

"Let's press on," said Blob. "I want to finish up here and get back to Aargh! and Ugh! before dark."

"How long will it take to get back?" said Blub.

"Seventy-five jars," said Blob. "But if we go into hyperjam we can make it three times as sticky."

"We'd better hyperjam it out of here then," said Blub.

"There's something big coming this way."

"Is it intelligent life?" said Blob.

"It's a mummosaurus," said Blub.

"Great blubbering blue blibbles!" said Blob.

"What's it going to do?"

"Cheese omelettes," said the mummosaurus, "with chips and baked beans."

"Careful," said Blob to Blub and Bleep, "this may be a trap."

"Chah! Chah! Chah!" said Bleep, stamping his feet and dancing around.

"You can't have chocolate cake until you've eaten your cheese omelette," said the mummosaurus.

The mummosaurus put the cheese omelettes on the table.

"Looks pretty good actually," said Blob.

"The mummosaurus is attacking the ship!" said Blub.

"It's tearing it apart," said Blob.

"What shall we do?" said Blub.

"Eat our cheese omelettes," said Blob, "and wait for a chance to escape."

"In what?" said Blub. "We've got no ship now."

"Don't panic," said Blob. "Maybe we can do a deal."

"Right you are," said the mummosaurus. "Eat your omelettes and your beans

12

and chips and then you can have your chocolate cake and then you can put your space ship back together."

"Chah!" said Bleep.

"That's it," said the mummosaurus. "Chocolate cake all round."

When Blob and Bleep had finished they thanked the mummosaurus.

"You're very welcome," said the mummosaurus. "Drop in any time you're in this part of the solar system."

"What do you call this planet?" said Blob when they had the space ship back together and were ready to blast off.

"We call it Earth," said the mummosaurus. "What do you call it?"

"We call it Plovsnat," said Blob. "In our language that means the place of the chocolate cake."

"Ready for blast off," said Blub.

Everybody kissed the mummosaurus goodbye.

"Blast off!" said Blob.

Off they blasted, roaring into space, and as they set their course for home they shouted their new battle cry,

"Three chahs for Aargh! Three chahs for Ugh!"

Three chahs for Aargh!
Three chahs for Ugh!

THIS IS THE BEAR

by Sarah Hayes
illustrated by Helen Craig

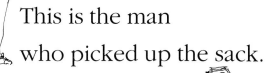

This is the man
who picked up the sack.

This is the driver
who would not come back.

This is the bear
who went to the dump
and fell on the pile
with a bit of a bump.

This is the bear
who fell in the bin.

This is the dog
who pushed him in.

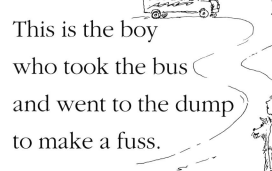

This is the boy
who took the bus
and went to the dump
to make a fuss.

This is the man
in an awful grump
who searched and searched
and searched the dump.

This is the bear
all lovely and clean
who did not say
just where he had been.

This is the bear
all cold and cross
who did not think
he was really lost.

This is the boy
who knew quite well,
but promised his friend
he would not tell.

This is the dog
who smelled the smell
of a bone and a tin
and a bear as well.

And this is the boy
who woke up in the night
and asked the bear
if he felt all right –
and was very surprised
when the bear shouted out,
"How soon can we have
another day out?"

This is the man
who drove them home –
the boy, the bear
and the dog with a bone.

JUST LIKE ARCHIE

by Niki Daly

Tom found a snail in the garden.

"What have you got there?" Mum asked.

"It's Archie," Tom said. "He's my pet."

Mum frowned and said, "I don't think snails make good pets."

Tom put Archie into a jam jar.

"I think he might like some fresh leaves,"

Mum said.

Tom ran back into the garden to

collect leaves.

While Tom was gone, Archie crawled

out of the jam jar and went for a walk.

He crawled around a corner and through a tunnel …

over a mountain …

and into

Tom's sneaker.

When Tom came in, he found the jar empty. "Where's Archie?" Tom asked.

"I told you snails don't make good pets," Mum said. But she helped him look anyway. They looked everywhere but they couldn't find Archie.

Then Tom saw a silvery trail going around a corner, through a tunnel, over a mountain … and into his sneaker.

"Here he is!" Tom shouted.

Tom decided to put Archie back in the garden. It made him feel a little sad.

Mum said, "Would you like a real pet, Tom?"

"Yes," said Tom. "Someone like Archie."

So Mum and Dad bought Tom a little white mouse. Tom called him Archie because he liked going for walks around the corner, through a tunnel, over a mountain … and into Tom's sneaker. Just like Archie!

All Fall Down

Singing all together,

bouncy,

by Helen Oxenbury

running round and round,

bouncy on the bed,

all fall down.

Bad Egg

by Sarah Hayes
illustrated by
Charlotte Voake

Humpty Dumpty
sat on a wall.
A horse came up to watch.
"Can you sit on this wall, horse?"
said Humpty Dumpty.
"Of course," said the horse.
And he did.

Then he wobbled
and wobbled, and
then he fell off.
Humpty Dumpty laughed.
"Tee hee," he said,
"you've hurt your knee."

Humpty Dumpty
sat on the wall.
Another horse
came up to watch.
"Can you stand
on this wall, horse?"
said Humpty Dumpty.
"Of course,"
said the horse.
And he did.

Then he wobbled
and wobbled, and
then he fell off.
Humpty Dumpty
laughed. "Oh dear," he
said, "you've
hurt your ear."

Humpty Dumpty
sat on the wall.
A man came up to watch.
"Can you stand
on one leg
on this wall, man?"
Humpty Dumpty said.
"Yes," said the man, "I can."
And he did.

Then he
wobbled and
wobbled, and
then he fell off.
Humpty Dumpty
laughed. "Ho ho," he
said, "you've
hurt your toe."

Humpty Dumpty
sat on the wall.
Another man came
up to watch.
"Can you stand
on one leg and
juggle with bricks
on this wall, man?"
Humpty Dumpty said.
"Well," said the man,
"I think I can."
And he did.

Then he wobbled
and wobbled, and
then he fell off.
Humpty Dumpty
laughed. "Go to bed,"
he said, "you've
hurt your head."

Humpty Dumpty
sat on the wall.
The King came up
to watch.
He saw his horses
and he saw his men.
And the King was terribly,
terribly cross.

"Come down,"
the King said. "Come
down from that wall."
But Humpty Dumpty
said nothing at all.
He stood on one leg
and juggled with bricks.
He did cartwheels
and headstands
and all sorts of tricks.

Then he wobbled
and wobbled, and
then he fell off.
CRASH!

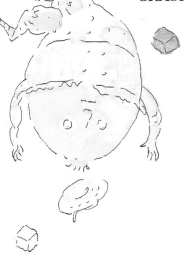

And all the King's horses,
and all the King's men…
put Humpty Dumpty
together again.
And Humpty said,
"After such a great fall
I'll never ever
climb back on
that wall."

But he did!

TALES *from* BARON MUNCHAUSEN

by Adrian Mitchell   illustrated by Patrick Benson

As for me, I rode off into the centre of Ceylon upon Never You Mind. As we paused at a river to drink, I thought I heard a rustling noise. Turning around I was interested to see an enormous lion.

He was striding towards me. His tongue lolled from his mouth. It was obvious that he wanted to eat me for lunch and Never You Mind for pudding.

What was to be done? My rifle was only loaded with swan-shot. This would kill nothing bigger than a small wombat.

I am well-known as a lover of animals. I decided to frighten the lion. I fired into the air. But the bang only angered him. He ran towards me at full speed.

I tried to run away. But the moment I turned from the lion I found myself face to face with a large crocodile. Its mouth was open wide. I could have walked inside without bending my head.

So, the crocodile was in front of me. The lion was behind me. On my left was a foaming river. On my right was a precipice. At the bottom of the precipice I could see a nest of green and yellow snakes.

I gave myself up for lost. The lion rose up onto his back legs. He was ready to pounce. At that second I tripped and fell to the ground. So the lion sprang over me.

For a long moment I lay still.

I expected to feel the claws of the lion in my hair and the jaws of the crocodile around my heels. Then there was an awful noise. I sat up and looked around.

Imagine my joy when I saw that the lion had jumped so far that he had jammed his head into the open mouth of the crocodile. They were struggling together, each of them trying to escape.

I drew my sword and cut off the lion's head with one stroke. Then, with the butt of my rifle, I drove the lion's head down the crocodile's throat. The crocodile died of suffocation – a brief, merciful death, I am pleased to say.

Some absurd versions of this story have been spread. In one of these, the lion jumps right down the crocodile's throat and is emerging at the

other end when I cut
off his head. This, of
course, is impossible.
I think it is shameful
that the truth should be
taken so lightly.

CAT and DOG

by David Lloyd   illustrated by Clive Scruton

Who walks out
through the back door?
Who walks pitter-pat
down the garden?
Who walks tip-toe
along the wall?

Cat.

Who jumps down
into the alley?
Who goes scritch-scratch
against the fence?

Who walks tall-tail between
the bottles?

Cat.

Who should watch out
round the corner?

Cat.

Watch out, cat!

Dog!

Quick, cat, quick!
Who runs snip-snap
round the corner?

Dog.

Quick, cat, quick!
Who runs snip-snap
round the corner,
between the bottles?
Getting closer.

Dog.

Quick, cat, quick!
Who runs snip-snap
down the alley?
Getting closer.
Getting closer.

Dog.

Snip! Snap!
Jump, cat!
Jump, dog!
Who falls back?

Dog!

Along the wall,
who walks tip-toe?
Up the garden,
who walks pitter-pat?
Through the back door,
who comes back?
Softly. Safely.

Cat.

Charlie Meadows

by Russell Hoban
illustrated by
Martin Baynton

Charlie Meadows had a paper round. His paper was an old and yellowed torn-off scrap of headline. BLEAK OUTLO, it said. Charlie carried it in a cleft stick. When the other meadow mice saw the paper coming they knew that it was Charlie with the news and weather.

Charlie got the weather from his grandmother, she had rheumatism and she always knew when it was going to rain. The news he picked up as he made his round. Charlie always made his round between midnight and three o'clock in the morning. Every time he went out his mother said to him, "Look out for Ephraim Owl or *you'll* be in the news, Charlie Meadows."

Charlie always said he would be careful but he was perhaps not quite so careful as he might have been, he was too fond of moonlight. He especially liked the full-moon nights in winter when the shadows were black on the snow and the frozen pond creaked and his whiskers were stiff with the cold. Sometimes he would skate on the pond and on the frozen stream that ran through the meadow and the wood.

One full-moon night Ephraim Owl was sitting in a tall pine that overlooked the pond. There had just been a fresh snowfall and the ice on the pond was white under the moon.

Ephraim ruffled his feathers and made himself bigger. "WHOOHOOHOO!" he hooted, and looked all round to see if anyone jumped up and ran.

"WHOOHOOHOOHOO!" he hooted again. Such a sudden sound, so strange! Even Ephraim wasn't sure if he had made it or if it had leapt out of the night all by itself.

When Charlie heard the hooting he was in the shadow of the pines on his way from Poverty Hollow to Frogtown Stump. Up he jumped and ran out into the whiteness of the frozen pond. His little black shadow began to dance, it kept changing its shape and Charlie had to dance and change his shape with it. The shadow of his cleft stick and paper grew long, grew short, spun round and round as he danced. Down swooped Ephraim from the tall pine, down he swooped on silent wings with outstretched talons. Just as he was going to grab Charlie he drew back his talons and flew up again. He wanted Charlie for his supper but he didn't want Charlie's little shadow to stop dancing.

He liked the way it whirled and changed its shape, he flew low over the ice and tried to make his shadow do the same, it seemed the proper thing to do with the moonlight.

Round and round went Charlie's shadow and Charlie, round and round went Ephraim's shadow and Ephraim. Ephraim's shadow got all mixed up with Charlie's shadow and Ephraim became confused. He sat down suddenly on the ice while everything went round and round him. That was when Charlie noticed Ephraim for the first time. He too became confused, he stopped dancing and stood absolutely still, trembling all over and staring at Ephraim.

Ephraim looked at Charlie's paper. "What's that?" he said.

"BLEAK OUTLO," said Charlie.

"What's a BLEAK OUTLO?" said Ephraim.

"It's a paper," said Charlie.

"I can see that it's a paper," said Ephraim. "But what does BLEAK OUTLO mean?"

"I don't know," said Charlie. "That's what it says on the paper."

"How do you know that's what it says?" said Ephraim.

"My grandmother told me," said Charlie.

"Oh," said Ephraim.

Ephraim began to think of supper again. He stood up and ruffled up all his feathers and made himself big. He spread his wings and leant low towards Charlie to show his ruffled-up back feathers and the tops of his wings so that Charlie could see how big he was. He snapped his bill and his yellow eyes stared straight at Charlie.

Charlie couldn't move, he stood there as if he were frozen to the spot, his little black shadow was perfectly motionless.

Ephraim looked at Charlie's shadow. "Oh well," he said, "never mind." He made himself regular-sized again. "You watch it next time," he said, and off he flew.

Charlie hurried on to Frogtown Stump. "BLEAK OUTLO news and weather," he said, "warm spell coming, rain and fog."

"What about the news?" said the Frogtown Stump mice.

"Ephraim Owl's out hunting by the pond," said Charlie.

"That's not news," said the Frogtown Stumpers.

"No," said Charlie, "I guess it isn't."

He never told what happened at the pond, he let that stay between him and Ephraim.

Till Owlyglass

by Michael Rosen   illustrated by Fritz Wegner

 One day Till arrived in the city of Luneburg. This time he thought he'd try his luck at being a doctor, so he practised talking and behaving like a doctor. And then he put up notices on all the church doors saying that he could cure every kind of illness that anyone ever had.

"No matter what you've got wrong with you," Till said, "I can make you better."

Of course he didn't know how to do any such thing, but people believed him and people came to see him. And when they came to see Till, he would look at their tongues, and feel their heads, and ask them questions. Then he would look really serious and say, "Um, ah, yes… I think you need a strong dose of warm water," and then the person would go away and drink warm water.

Sometimes they got better, perhaps because of the warm water, perhaps because they were going to get better anyway, or perhaps just because they believed that Till was a great doctor.

One day the man who was in charge of the town hospital came to see Till. "I hear that you are a great and wonderful doctor," he said, "and you can cure all illnesses. My hospital is very full at the moment, too full in fact. Do you think you could come and help me?"

So Till said, "Look, if I can cure all your patients in one day, so that there is nobody left in your hospital, will you give me two hundred pieces of gold?"

"If you can do it," said the man, "you can have the money."

"Right," said Till, "but first I'll have to go and see your patients to see what I've got to do to make them better."

The next day Till went off to the hospital, and there he walked from bed to bed looking at each patient. He also had something to say to each patient. He went and whispered in each patient's ear, "I want to tell you a secret, but you mustn't tell anyone else. You're very ill, but I know how to cure you. I want to give you back your health and strength, but to do this, I've got to take one of you, whoever is the *most* ill, and I've got to burn this really ill person down to powder. Then I'll mix the powder into a drink, give you the drink, and when you've drunk it you'll be better. I'm going to take the one who is the *most* ill to turn into powder, all right?"

Till told each patient that this was what he was going to do. The next morning Till told the man in charge of the hospital that he had cured everybody. "I can't believe it," said the man.

"Well," said Till, "all you have to do is stand at the door of your hospital and say that if any patients are feeling better, they can pack their bags and go."

So that's what the man did. He stood in the hospital doorway and called out, "All of you who are feeling better, take up your bags and go."

Well, you can guess what happened. All the patients were so afraid of being turned into powder and fed to the others that they got up out of bed and rushed out the door as fast as their legs would carry them. The man in charge could scarcely believe his eyes.

"All better? So soon?" he said. Then he went to the hospital treasury and gave Till two hundred pieces of gold.

A few days later some of the sick people started coming back. "What's the matter?" said the man in charge. "Didn't I hire a famous doctor to make you all better? Why have you come back?"

When they told him what Till had said to them, he realised he had been tricked. But the two hundred pieces of gold were gone and there was nothing he could do about it. Then he thought to himself, Well, well, well, Owlyglass didn't do any worse than plenty of real doctors I have heard of, who couldn't cure anybody either.

Tell Us a Story

by Allan Ahlberg
illustrated by
Colin McNaughton

Two little boys
climbed up
to bed.

"Tell us a story, Dad,"
they said.
"Right!" said Dad.

32

The Pig

"There was once a pig
who ate too much
and got so big
he couldn't sit down,
he couldn't bend.

So he ate standing up
and got bigger –
The End!"

"That story's no good,
Dad," the little boys said.
"Tell us a better one
instead."
"Right!" said Dad.

The Cat

"There was once a cat
who ate so much
and got so fat

he split his fur
which he had to mend
with a sewing machine
and a zip – The End!"

"That story's too mad,
Dad," the little boys said
"Tell us another one
instead."
"Right!" said Dad.

The Horse

There once was a horse
who ate too much and
died, of course –
The End!"

He's not dead!

I'm just horsing around!

That story's too sad,
Dad," the little boys said.
Tell us a nicer one
instead."
Right!" said Dad.

The Cow

"There once was a cow
who ate so much
that even now
she fills two fields

I've got four stomachs to fill!

and blocks a road,
and when they milk her
she has to be towed!
She wins gold cups
and medals too,
for the creamiest milk
and the *loudest* moo!"

"Now that's the end,"
said Dad. "No more."
And he shut his
eyes and
began to
snore.

Then the two little boys
climbed out of bed
and crept downstairs

to their Mum instead.

The End

Dad's Back

by Jan Ormerod

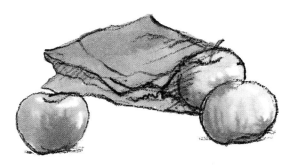

Dad's back with jingling keys,
warm gloves,
a cold nose,
a long, long scarf
and apples in a bag.
Dad's back with a game,
a chase
and a tickle.

TEN IN THE BED

There were **T E N** in the bed
and the little one said,
"Roll over, roll over!"
So they all rolled over
and Hedgehog fell out …

BUMP!

There were **N I N E** in the bed
and the little one said,
"Roll over, roll over!"
So they all rolled over
and Zebra fell out …

OUCH!

There were **E I G H T** in the bed
and the little one said,
"Roll over, roll over!"
So they all rolled over
and Ted fell out …

THUMP!

36

There were **S E V E N** in the bed
and the little one said,
"Roll over, roll over!"
So they all rolled over
and Croc fell out …

THUD!

There were **S I X** in the bed
and the little one said,
"Roll over, roll over!"
So they all rolled over
and Rabbit fell out …

BONK!

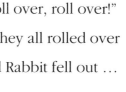

There were **F I V E** in the bed
and the little one said,
"Roll over, roll over!"
So they all rolled over
and Mouse fell out …

DINK!

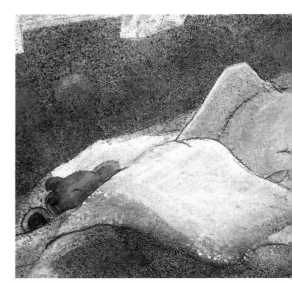

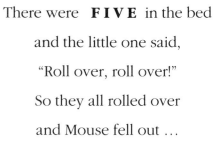

by Penny Dale

There were **FOUR** in the bed
and the little one said,
"Roll over, roll over!"
So they all rolled over
and Nelly fell out …

CRASH!

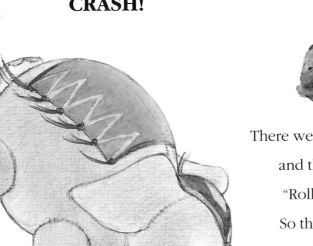

There were **THREE** in the bed
and the little one said,
"Roll over, roll over!"
So they all rolled over
and Bear fell out …

SLAM!

There were **TWO** in the bed
and the little one said,
"Roll over, roll over!"
So they all rolled over
and Sheep fell out …

DONK!

There was **ONE** in the bed
and the little one said,
"I'm cold! I miss you!"

So they all came back
and jumped into bed –
Hedgehog, Mouse, Nelly, Zebra,
Ted, the little one, Rabbit, Croc,
Bear and Sheep.

Ten in the bed,
all fast asleep.

Can't You Sleep, Little Bear?

by Martin Waddell   illustrated by Barbara Firth

 Once there were two bears. Big Bear and Little Bear. Big Bear is the big bear, and Little Bear is the little bear. They played all day in the bright sunlight. When night came, and the sun went down, Big Bear took Little Bear home to the Bear Cave.

Big Bear put Little Bear to bed in the dark part of the cave. "Go to sleep, Little Bear," he said. And Little Bear tried. Big Bear settled in the Bear Chair and read his Bear Book, by the light of the fire. But Little Bear couldn't get to sleep.

"Can't you sleep, Little Bear?" asked Big Bear, putting down his Bear Book (which was just getting to the interesting part) and padding over to the bed. "I'm scared," said Little Bear. "Why are you scared, Little Bear?" asked Big Bear. "I don't like the dark," said Little Bear. "What dark?" said Big Bear. "The dark all around us," said Little Bear.

Big Bear looked, and he saw that the dark part of the cave was very dark, so he went to the Lantern Cupboard and took out the tiniest lantern that was there. Big Bear lit the tiniest lantern, and put it near to Little Bear's bed. "There's a tiny light to stop you being scared, Little Bear," said Big Bear. "Thank you, Big Bear," said Little Bear, cuddling up in the glow. "Now go to sleep, Little Bear," said Big Bear, and he padded back to the Bear Chair and settled down to read the Bear Book, by the light of the fire.

Little Bear tried to go to sleep, but he couldn't. "Can't you sleep, Little Bear?" yawned Big Bear, putting down his Bear Book (with just four pages to go to the interesting bit) and padding over to the bed. "I'm scared," said Little Bear. "Why are you scared, Little Bear?" asked Big Bear. "I don't like the dark," said Little Bear. "What dark?" asked Big Bear. "The dark all around us," said Little Bear. "But I brought you a lantern!" said Big Bear. "Only a tiny-weeny one," said Little Bear. "And there's lots of dark!"

Big Bear looked, and he saw that Little Bear was quite right, there was still lots of dark. So Big Bear went to the Lantern Cupboard and took out a bigger lantern. Big Bear lit the lantern and put it beside the other one.

"Now go to sleep, Little Bear," said Big Bear and he padded back to the Bear Chair and settled down to read the Bear Book, by the light of the fire.

Little Bear tried and tried to go to sleep, but he couldn't.

"Can't you sleep, Little Bear?" grunted Big Bear, putting down his Bear Book (with just three pages to go) and padding over to the bed.

"I'm scared," said Little Bear. "Why are you scared, Little Bear?" asked Big Bear. "I don't like the dark," said Little Bear. "What dark?" asked Big Bear. "The dark all around us," said Little Bear. "But I brought you two lanterns!" said Big Bear. "A tiny one and a bigger one!" "Not much bigger," said Little Bear. "And there's still lots of dark."

Big Bear thought about it, and then he went to the Lantern Cupboard and took out the Biggest Lantern of Them All, with two handles and a bit of chain. He hooked the lantern up above Little Bear's bed. "I've brought you the Biggest Lantern of Them All!" he told Little Bear. "That's to stop you being scared!" "Thank you, Big Bear," said Little Bear, curling up in the glow and watching the shadows dance. "Now go to sleep, Little Bear," said Big Bear and he padded back to the Bear Chair and settled down to read the Bear Book, by the light of the fire.

Little Bear tried and tried and tried to go to sleep, but he couldn't.

"Can't you sleep, Little Bear?" groaned Big Bear, putting down his Bear Book (with just two pages to go) and padding over to the bed. "I'm scared," said Little Bear. "Why are you scared, Little Bear?" asked Big Bear. "I don't like the dark," said Little Bear. "What dark?" asked Big Bear. "The dark all around us," said Little Bear.

"But I brought you the Biggest Lantern of Them All, and there isn't any dark left," said Big Bear. "Yes, there is!" said Little Bear. "There is, out there!" And he pointed out of the Bear Cave, at the night.

Big Bear saw that Little Bear was right. Big Bear was very puzzled. All the lanterns in the world couldn't light up the dark outside. Big Bear thought about it for a long time, and then he said, "Come on, Little Bear." "Where are we going?" asked Little Bear. "Out!" said Big Bear. "Out into the darkness?" said Little Bear. "Yes!" said Big Bear. "But I'm scared of the dark!" said Little Bear. "No need to be!" said Big Bear, and he took Little Bear by the paw and led him out from the cave into the night and it was...

DARK! "Ooooh! I'm scared," said Little Bear, cuddling up to Big Bear. Big Bear lifted Little Bear, and cuddled him, and said, "Look at the dark, Little Bear." And Little Bear looked. "I've brought you the moon, Little Bear," said Big Bear. "The bright yellow moon, and all the twinkly stars."

But Little Bear didn't say anything, for he had gone to sleep, warm and safe in Big Bear's arms. Big Bear carried Little Bear back into the Bear Cave, fast asleep, and he settled down with Little Bear on one arm and the Bear Book on the other, cosy in the Bear Chair by the fire.

And Big Bear read the Bear Book right to...

T H E   E N D

THE TROUBLE WITH ELEPHANTS

by Chris Riddell

The trouble with elephants is… they spill the bath water when they get in and they leave a pink elephant ring when they get out. They take all the bedclothes and they snore elephant snores which rattle the window panes. The only way to wake a sleeping elephant is to shout "Mouse!" in its ear. Then it will slide down the banisters to breakfast. Elephants travel four in a car – two in the front and two in the back. You can always tell when an elephant is visiting because there'll be a car outside with three elephants in it. Sometimes elephants ride bicycles, but not very often.

The trouble with
elephants is that
on elephant
picnics they eat all
the buns before you've
finished your first one.
Elephants drink their lemonade
through their trunks and if you're
not looking they
drink yours too.
On elephant
picnics they play
games like leap-
elephant and
skipping, which they're good at.
And sometimes
they play hide
and seek, which
they're not very
good at.

The trouble with
elephants is...
well, there are
all sorts of
troubles...
all sorts of
troubles...
but the real trouble is...
you can't help but
love them.

jangle twang

toot clash

jangle

sing

by John Burningham

twang

pluck

boom

FUR

by Jan Mark
illustrated by
Charlotte Voake

Thin Kitty grew fat.
She made a nest in my hat,
another in the kitchen cupboard,
and a third on Mum's skirt.
But she liked the hat nest best.
All night she purred.
And now my hat is full of fur.

Kittens!

JACK AND THE COMBINE

by Heather Maisner • illustrated by Norman Johnson

On the first day of the harvest Jack began to sing as soon as Farmer Thomson and his daughter Rosemary fitted the cutting and threshing machine to his back. The animals and tractors watched him set off down the drive.

"I wish I were cutting the fields again," sighed Sam, the old tractor.

"So do I," croaked Rufus the cart-horse. "I used to love harvest time."

"I hate it," moaned Kate, the red tractor. "I get so tired and Jack works much too fast."

Out in the main road Jack kept close to the hedge. He went past the sugar-beet and by the forest, round the pond, through the gate and into the field.

Then up and down and up and down he drove, cutting the corn and threshing the corn, and singing his song as he went:

"I'm a tractor,
my name is Jack,
I live in Thomson's Yard.
I can go forward
and I can go back,
I'm happiest working hard."

"Do slow down," Kate panted behind him. "I'll never keep up with the bales."

"Of course you will," laughed Jack.

"I'm hot and sore and covered with midges," she said.

"Sing and you'll soon forget," said Jack.

By evening the field was dotted with bales. Aching and tired, the tractors crawled back to the yard.

"Tomorrow we start

over the hill," said Jack. "Oh no." Kate's eyes began to close. "I wish I could sleep for a week." "I wish I could work all night," said Jack. But soon he too fell asleep.

CRUNCH CRUNCH CRUNCH

Jack opened one eye. It was still dark.

CRUNCH CRUNCH CRUNCH

"What is it?" Kate whispered, pressing against him. An enormous thing was moving down the drive.
"It's the end of the world," groaned Sam.
"Cock-a-doodle-doo! Cock-a-doodle-doo!" cried the cockerel. The cart-horse neighed and stamped his hoofs. The pigs snorted, the cows

mooed. The dog ran out into the drive and howled. But the monster moved steadily towards them.

CRUNCH CRUNCH CRUNCH

Jack stepped boldly forward.
"Stop!" he said. "Who are you? What do you want?" The monster stood still and licked its lips. Its

nostrils flared. It opened its mouth and a voice boomed out.
"I'm Harold, Harold the combine. I've come to cut Farmer Thomson's corn." The farmyard was silent.
"That's my job," said Jack. "I cut the corn."
"Was your job," said the combine. "Now it's mine." When the sun was high in the sky, Harold moved down the drive with Farmer Thomson.

"He hasn't got a scratch on him," said Kate. "He probably doesn't know how to cut the fields."
"Oh yes I do," said Harold. "I can do everything." He swung out into the main road and his body filled the whole space from one side to the other. Along the main road and past the sugar-beet, by the forest and round the pond, up the hill and through the gate he lurched.
Then up and down and up and down he rolled, cutting and threshing and cleaning the corn.

Back at the yard Jack stood silently. For the first time in his life he hadn't sung his song.
"You can do my job," whispered Kate. "You can do the baling."
"I expect Harold does that too," said Jack. "I guess I'll be sitting in the yard all day now, unless I'm sold for scrap." A large tear rolled down his cheek. "Trouble is, I don't know what to do if I'm not working."

Suddenly Rosemary ran up the drive and began to fit the large trailer to Jack. Without saying a word they set off for the fields. Along the road and past the sugar-beet, by the forest and round the pond, up the hill and through the gate they hurried.
Harold stood absolutely still in the middle of the field. He'd stopped working.
"What's up?" asked Jack.

"Why have you stopped?"
"The grain needs emptying," said Harold.
"Can't you take care of that yourself?" asked Jack.
"Of course not," Harold snorted. "I'm needed here. I can't go trundling back to the yard every twenty minutes, can I?"
As the grain spilt from Harold's tank into the trailer, Jack asked, "What do you do after the harvest, Harold, when all the corn's cut?"
"Nothing. I rest."
"You mean you don't do anything all year?"
"That's right. I preserve my energy for the harvest."
Jack moved back along the road with the trailer full of corn. If Harold spent most of the year resting, he wouldn't be taking Jack's place after all. There was

the ploughing and hedge-cutting, the digging and shovelling, the fetching and carrying and oh so many things to do. Slowly he began to sing:

*"I'm a tractor,
my name is Jack,
I live in Thomson's Yard.
I can go forward
and I can go back,
I'm happiest working hard."*

AN AWFUL LOT

Monday's child is red and spotty,
 Tuesday's child won't use the potty.
      Wednesday's child won't go to bed,
       Thursday's child will not be fed.

HOW MANY STARS?

When I was a boy
I would ask my dad:
"How many stars
 are there hanging
 in the sky?"
"More than enough, son,
More than I could say.
Enough to keep you
 counting
Till your dying day."

When I was a boy
I would ask my dad:
"How many fishes
 are there swimming
 in the sea?"
"More than enough, son,
More than I could say.
Enough to keep you
 counting
Till your dying day."

When I was a boy
I would ask my dad:
"How many creepy-crawlies
 are there
 in the world?"
"More than enough, son,
More than I could say.
Enough to keep you
 counting
Till your dying day."

It seemed like there wasn't anything my dad didn't know.

You don't frighten me!

DON'T PUT SUGAR IN MY TEA, MUM

Don't put sugar in my tea, Mum.
 Don't put sugar in my tea.
  I'm already fat,
   So that's enough of that.
    Don't put sugar in my tea.

by Colin McNaughton

Friday's child breaks all his toys,
  Saturday's child makes an awful noise.

And the child that's born on the seventh day
  Is a pain in the neck like the rest, OK!

I AM A JOLLY GIANT

I am a jolly giant,
  I have no cares or woes,
    If you don't give me
      all your cash,
        I'll punch you
          in the nose.

SHORT SHARP SHOCK

If your children are ever unruly,
(Of course this might never happen),
Just tell them to kindly behave themselves,
Then reach over quickly and slap 'em!

I DON'T WANT TO GO INTO SCHOOL

I don't want to go into school today, Mum,
I don't feel like schoolwork today.
Oh, don't make me go into school today, Mum,
Oh, please let me stay home and play.

But you must go to school, my cherub, my lamb.
If you don't it will be a disaster.
How would they manage without you, my sweet,
After all, you are the headmaster!

DUNCE

I always try my hardest,
I always do my best.
It's just that I don't seem to be
As clever as the rest.

53

UNDER THE BED

by Michael Rosen   *illustrated by Quentin Blake*

Messing About

"Do you know what?"
said Jumping John.
"I had a bellyache
and now it's gone."

"Do you know what?"
said Kicking Kirsty.
"All this jumping
has made me thirsty."

"Do you know what?"
said Mad Mickey.
"I sat in some glue
and I feel all sticky."

"Do you know what?"
said Fat Fred.
"You can't see me,
I'm under the bed."

After Dark

Outside after dark
trains hum and traffic lights wink
after dark, after dark.

In here after dark
curtains shake and cupboards creak
after dark, after dark.

Under the covers after dark
I twiddle my toes and hug my pillow
after dark, after dark.

These Two Children

There were these two children
and they were in bed and it was
time they were asleep.

But they were making a huge noise,
shouting, yelling and screaming.
"Look at me!" "Look at you!"
"Let's go mad!" "Yes, let's go mad!"

Their dad heard them and
he shouted up to them,
"Stop the noise! Stop the noise!
If you don't stop the noise, I'm
coming upstairs and I'll give
you a bit of real trouble."

Everything went quiet.

A few minutes later one of the
children called out,
"Dad, Dad, when you come up to give
us a bit of real trouble, can you bring
us up a drink of water as well?"

Nat and Anna

Anna was in her room.
Nat was outside the door.
Anna didn't want Nat to come in.
Nat said, "Anna? Anna? Can I come in?"
Anna said, "I'm not in."

Nat went away.
Anna was still in her room.
Nat came back.
Nat said, "How did you say you're not in?
You must be in if you said you're not in."
Anna said, "I'm not in."
Nat said, "I'm coming in to see if you're in."
Anna said, "You won't find me because I'm not in."
Nat said, "I'm coming in."

Nat went in.
Nat said, "There you are. You are in."
Anna said, "Nat, where are you?
Where are you, Nat?"
Nat said, "I'm here."
Anna said, "I can't see you, Nat. Where are you?"
Nat said, "I'm here. Look."
Anna said, "Sorry, Nat. I can't see you."
Nat said, "Here I am. I'm going to scream, Anna.
Then you'll see me."
Anna said, "Where are you, Nat?"
Nat said, *"Yaaaaaaaaaaaaaaaaaaaa!"*
Anna said, "I can hear you, Nat. But I can't see you."
Nat said, "Right. I'm going out. Then you'll see me."

Nat went out.
Nat said, "Anna? Anna, can you see me now?"
Anna said, "No, of course I can't, you're outside."
Nat said, "Can I come in and see you then?"
Anna said, "But I'm not in."
Nat went away screaming.
He didn't come back.

55

Out and About

by Shirley Hughes

The Grass House

The grass house
Is my private place.
Nobody can see me
In the grass house.
Feathery plumes
Meet over my head.
Down here,
In the green, there are:
Seeds
Weeds
Stalks
Pods
And tiny little flowers.

Only the cat
And some busy, hurrying ants
Know where my grass house is.

Mudlarks

I like mud.
The slippy, sloppy, squelchy kind,
The slap-it-into-pies kind.
Stir it up in puddles,
Slither and slide.
I *do* like mud.

Wind

I like the wind.
The soft, summery, gentle kind,
The gusty, blustery, fierce kind.
Ballooning out the curtains,
Blowing things about,
Wild and wilful everywhere.
I *do* like the wind.

Seaside

Sand in the sandwiches,
Sand in the tea,
Flat, wet sand running
Down to the sea.
Pools full of seaweed,
Shells and stones,
Damp bathing suits
And ice-cream cones.
Waves pouring in
To a sand-castle moat.
Mend the defences!
Now we're afloat!
Water's for splashing,
Sand is for play,
A day by the sea
Is the best kind of day.

Water

I like water.
The shallow, splashy, paddly kind,
The hold-on-tight-it's-deep kind.
Slosh it out of buckets,
Spray it all around.
I *do* like water.

Sick

Hot, cross, aching head,
Prickly, tickly, itchy bed.
Piles of books and toys and puzzles
Heavy on my feet,
Pillows thrown all anyhow,
Wrinkles in the sheet.
Sick of medicine, lemonade,
Soup spooned from a cup.
When will I be *better?*
When can I *get up?*

Sand

I like sand.
The run-between-your-fingers kind,
The build-it-into-castles kind.
Mountains of sand meeting the sky,
Flat sand, going on for ever.
I *do* like sand.

The Dancing Class

by Helen 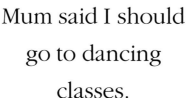 *Oxenbury*

Mum said I should
go to dancing
classes.

"We'll take these tights.
She'll soon grow into them."

"We'll just make
your hair tidy like the others."

"Heads up, tummies in, knees straight and
point your toes," the teacher said.

60

"Don't cry, you'll soon learn.
I'll show you the right way
to tie up your shoes."

"You danced very well,"
the teacher told me. "Will you
come again next week?"

"This is what we do, Mum.
Watch. I'll do the gallop all the way home."

FIVE MINUTES' PEACE

by Jill Murphy

The children were having breakfast. This was not a pleasant sight.
Mrs Large took a tray from the cupboard.
She set it with a teapot, a milk jug, her favourite cup and saucer, a plate of marmalade toast and a leftover cake from yesterday. She stuffed the morning paper into her pocket and sneaked off towards the door.
"Where are you going with that tray, Mum?" asked Laura.
"To the bathroom," said Mrs Large.

"Why?" asked the other two children.
"Because I want five minutes' peace from you lot," said Mrs Large.
"That's why."

"Can we come?" asked Lester as they trailed up the stairs behind her.
"No," said Mrs Large, "you can't."
"What shall we do then?" asked Laura.
"You can play," said Mrs Large. "Downstairs. By yourselves. And keep an eye on the baby."
"I'm not a baby," muttered the little one.

Mrs Large ran a deep, hot bath. She emptied half a bottle of bath foam into the water, plonked on her bath-hat and got in.
She poured herself a cup of tea and lay back with her eyes closed.
It was heaven.

"Can I play you my tune?" asked Lester.
Mrs Large opened one eye.
"Must you?" she asked.
"I've been practising," said Lester. "You told me to. Can I? Please, just for one minute."
"Go on then," sighed Mrs Large.
So Lester played. He played "Twinkle, Twinkle, Little Star" three and a half times.
In came Laura. "Can I read you a page from my reading book?" she asked.
"No, Laura," said Mrs Large. "Go on, all of you, off downstairs."

"You let Lester play his tune," said Laura. "I heard. You like him better than me. It's not fair."
"Go on then. Just one page."
So Laura read. She read four and a half pages of "Little Red Riding Hood".
In came the little one with a trunkful of toys.
"For you!" he beamed, flinging them all into the bath water.
"Thank you, dear," said Mrs Large weakly.
"Can I see the cartoons in the paper?" asked Laura.
"Can I have the cake?" asked Lester.
"Can I get in with you?" asked the little one.
Mrs Large groaned.

In the end they all got in. The little one was in such a hurry that he forgot to take off his pyjamas.

Mrs Large got out. She dried herself, put on her dressing-gown and headed for the door.
"Where are you going now, Mum?" asked Laura.
"To the kitchen," said Mrs Large.
"Why?" asked Lester.
"Because I want five minutes' peace from you lot," said Mrs Large. "That's why." And off she went downstairs, where she had three minutes and forty-five seconds of peace before they all came to join her.

H. Prince

by Dick King-Smith

illustrated by Martin Honeysett

There was once a frog named
H. Prince. He lived in a
dirty duck pond with his
mother, Mrs Prince, and his
father, Mr Prince.
H. Prince often wondered what
the H stood for. Was he Henry? Was
he Herbert? Was he Humphrey?
"What does H stand for?" he asked his
mother one day.
But she only answered, "Hop it!"
He went to look for his father.
"What does H stand for?" he asked.
But his father only said, "Hop it!"
H. Prince was not very happy about this.
He blinked his eyes and his mouth
turned down at the corners.
But then he made up his mind.
He had to know what H stood for.
So he decided to leave home and find out.
He hopped out of the duck pond and
found himself in a field.
He hopped out of the field and found
himself by a road.
H. Prince hopped off down the road.
Soon he met a cat strolling along the road.

"Excuse me," said H. Prince politely.
"What does H stand for?"
"Hop it!" said the cat,
and hissed at the frog.
Next he met a dog
trotting along the road.
"Excuse me," said H. Prince
politely. "What does H stand for?"
"Hop it!" said the dog, and
growled at the frog.
Then he met a girl on a bike pedalling
along the road.
"Excuse me," said H. Prince politely
once again.
"What does H stand for?"
"Hop it!" said the girl on the bike, and
rang her bell at the frog.
Last of all he met a man driving a big lorry.
It was going fast and before H. Prince
could open his mouth, the man sounded
the horn and shouted at the frog.
"HOP IT!" he bellowed at the
top of his voice.
H. Prince hopped it, just in time.
He was not very happy about this.
He blinked his eyes and his mouth turned
down at the corners.
Sadly he hopped off the road and found
himself in a garden.
He hopped down the garden and found
himself by a goldfish pool.
It was not a bit like the dirty duck pond.

It was a beautiful goldfish pool, covered in beautiful water-lilies.
On one of the water-lilies sat a beautiful frog.
"Excuse me," H. Prince said to her.
"I wonder if you can help me."
He took a deep breath.
"What does H stand for?" he said.
"Why do you ask?" she said.
"Because my name is H. Prince," said H. Prince, "and I do not know what H stands for."
"I do," she said.
H. Prince blinked his eyes and his mouth turned down at the corners. I know what she will say, he thought sadly.

She will say what Mother and Father said. She will say what the cat and the dog and the girl on the bike and the man in the lorry said. She will say, "Hop it!" He waited but the frog did not speak.

She only gazed at him with her beautiful bulgy eyes.
H. Prince took another deep breath.
"What does H stand for?" he said.
"H," said the beautiful frog, "stands for Handsome."
H. Prince was very happy about this. His eyes shone and his mouth turned up at the corners.
"Yes," she said, "you are my very own Handsome Prince. Hop in!"
So H. Prince hopped in, and they lived happily ever after.

HERBERT THE CHICKEN

by Ivor Cutler
illustrated by Patrick Benson

When Herbert woke on Monday he found he had become a chicken, and flew downstairs. "Mum! Mum! I'm a chicken!" he squawked. "That's nice, Herbert," she laughed, and held up a mirror for him to look into.

Herbert laughed too. "Shall I go to school?"

"Why not?" said she, placing a dish of corn upon the tablecloth. Clutching the rim with his claws, he pecked the plate clean then flew upstairs for his satchel.

When he returned, his mother popped a plastic bag of corn into his brown canvas schoolbag.

"Peck a hole in it at lunch," she said, kissing his little yellow beak.

Herbert flew to school, straight through an open window and sat on his seat. The class gasped at Herbert when they entered.

"Sit down, everybody," called Mr Balloon, the teacher, and turned to Herbert.

"Well Herbert, you're a chicken."

Herbert flew round the room and returned to his place. The class watched with shining eyes and smiling lips, listening to the fluttering.

"Take out your diaries," said Mr Balloon quietly. The class started writing. Herbert dipped his beak into a pot of Brown's ink that the teacher placed by his feathers and wrote –
Today I am a chicken.
It is lovely to be light.
I am very happy.

At playtime, the school gathered round in the playground.

"How did you become a chicken?" Annie asked.

But Herbert had no answer.

"I just became one."

"Will you always be one?" Annie asked.

Herbert and Annie were in love.

He wagged his wings.

"I've no idea. I've never been one before."

The boys drifted away for a game of football. Herbert joined them. They picked sides and Herbert played centre forward. He discovered that he had a strong kick and scored three goals. The other team said it wasn't fair, so he switched sides and scored three goals for them. Then the whistle blew and they returned to the classroom. Painting time. Herbert posed on Mr Balloon's head. When they finished, the children fixed their paintings to the wall with sticky tape. What a large head Mr Balloon had.

Then the lunch bell rang. Herbert stayed in the classroom and pecked at his corn.

Annie kept him company, pecking at her sandwiches. "You look tired, Herbert," she said, peering at him. "It's hard being a chicken," he sighed, "I think I'll go home to bed. Goodbye, Annie." and hovering, pecked her lip slightly. Then he flew slowly round the room for a last look, and out the window.

Annie watched him go till he was a dot (·) then sat at her desk and peeled an orange. "I'm home!" clucked Herbert as he flew into his bedroom. Nobody was in, so he lay on the bed and went to sleep. At five, he woke and walked downstairs for tea. "Hey! I'm a boy again!" he called. "A good thing!" said his mother. "It's boiled egg for tea." And they both laughed.

The Hidden House

by Martin Waddell   illustrated by Angela Barrett

In a little house, down a little lane, lived an old man. His name was Bruno. He was very lonely in the little house, so he made wooden dolls to keep him company. He made three of them. The knitting one is Maisie, the one with the spade is Ralph, and the one with the pack on his back is Winnaker.

They sat on Bruno's window ledge and watched him working in his garden, growing potatoes and cabbages and parsnips and beans. Bruno talked to them sometimes, but not very much. They were wooden dolls and they couldn't talk back, and Bruno wasn't stupid. The dolls didn't talk, but I *think* they were happy.

One day Bruno went away and didn't come back. Everything changed, slowly. Wild things covered the lane and climbed all over Bruno's fence. Brambles choked the garden, and ivy crept in through the window of the little house and spread about inside. A pale tree grew in the kitchen.

Maisie and Ralph and Winnaker watched it happen from their window ledge and they got dusty. They watched and watched, until the spiders spun up their window so that there was nothing left to see but webs. They didn't say anything, because they were wooden dolls, but I *think* they were lonely.

A mouse came by and nibbled Ralph's spade. A beetle lived in Maisie's basket for a day and then it went away. An ant explored Winnaker but didn't find anything. Slowly, very slowly (it took years and years and years) Bruno's little house disappeared in the middle of green things. It was still there, but nobody could see it. The house was hidden, and Maisie and Ralph and Winnaker were hidden inside it. I think they were watching. There was a lot to see in the hidden house.

The house filled up with ants and beetles, mice and toads and creepy-crawlies, until it was fuller than it had ever been. Bees buzzed up the chimney, where the smoke used to be. The little house grew warm and smelly with decay, but it was full of things happening. Maisie and Ralph and Winnaker got damp and mildewed and turned a bit green, but I don't think they minded too much.

Then a man came down the lane and found the little house by poking his way in through the branches. He didn't spot Maisie and Ralph and Winnaker, because they were hidden in the ivy. He liked the little house. Next day he came again with his wife and daughter, and they explored the house and the garden, and liked it very much. They said they'd come back, but a long time

went by and they didn't come. The hidden house had been forgotten again, and I *think* the wooden dolls were sad.

A whole winter passed and the house was covered in snow. Lots of things came in from the wood and hid there, away from the cold.

Then, in the spring, the man came back with his wife and his little girl, and he brought a big axe. He cleared away the wildness round the little house. The man and his wife and the little girl cleaned and cleared and hammered and nailed and painted and washed and brushed and *did* until everything was lovely.

The little girl found Maisie and Ralph and Winnaker. She got her paintbrush and painted them. Then she set them on the window ledge, looking out at the garden. The garden was filled with flowers. "There you are!" said the little girl. "A whole new world to look at." "A whole new family for them to look after," said the woman. "Our family," said the man, and he hugged his wife and daughter.

Maisie and Ralph and Winnaker didn't say a thing. They couldn't. They were wooden dolls. But now they had a whole family to live with, and I *think* they were happy again.

HOB AND BOGGART

by William Mayne   illustrated by Patrick Benson

Who lit a twiggy fire in the ashes of the hearth and filled the house with smoke in the middle of the night? Mr asks the question, Mrs wants to know. Boy and Girl did not do it and cannot tell. Budgie knows and shouts it out. Baby sees and yells the name, but no one understands. "We'll go back to bed," says Mr. "I hope it's not your friend." Boy and Girl know how kindly Hob lives in his cutch or cupboard in the stairs. They know he did no such thing. "No," says Hob. "But I'm about. Hob is where he thinks he is." Mr and Mrs and Boy and Girl go back to bed. "I saw it, I saw it," says Budgie. Hob jumps up and makes a face at her.

He thinks Budgie is a noise and not a thing. He is quiet himself and does not like a noise. "Who is it?" he asks. But Budgie tucks her head under her wing and will not reply. Hob goes to ask Baby. "Wug, wug, wug," says Baby. Only Baby understands. Hob makes a face at it, and Baby laughs. Hob goes to find out for himself. He listens. Something bumps about the house. Hob hears the milk go sour. Something rattles at a door. Hob hears the bread go mouldy. Something shuffles across a floor. Hob hears the butter going wrong. Treading down the stairs he hears a scratching down below.

There is something climbing into his cutch, his living place. Hob is angry now. He goes right down.

He thinks he knows what this thing is. Budgie has fainted quite away, her feathers turning white. "It made a face at me," she croaks. "It's one of those," says Hob. "Hob thinks we'll have a fight." There, climbing into the cutch, is a fat and ugly Boggart with really wicked eyes, bringing trouble and noise to Hob's own lucky house. "Goodnight Hob," says Boggart. "You'll have to move." But Hob knows how to deal with Boggart.

Hob wheels him away. "What a trick," says Boggart. "They don't want me and here I am." "What a trick," says Hob. "Here we are," and tips the barrow in the river, box, Boggart, and all, and they float away. "Wet house," says Boggart, and Hob says, "Goodbye."

Hob goes home to see what Boy and Girl had left him. He hopes it is not clothes, or he will have to go. "If they cover Hob's back, he's off down the track," he says. But they left a twist of baccy. He smokes it by the chimney. "Home, sweet home," he says, among kindly folk.

"We're all off," he says cheerfully. "We're flitting, don't you know. We're doing it to trick you." "Silly Hob to tell me, then," says Boggart, climbing out. "Where do we go?"

"Wait a bit," said Hob, and out he goes for a wheelbarrow and puts a box on it. "Room for you in here," says Hob, and Boggart clambers in, mean and greedy.

OUR MAMMOTH

by Adrian Mitchell
illustrated by Priscilla Lamont

We are the Gumble Twins,
Bing and Saturday Gumble.
Bing is a gloomy boy.
Saturday is a cheerful girl.
We get along fine.

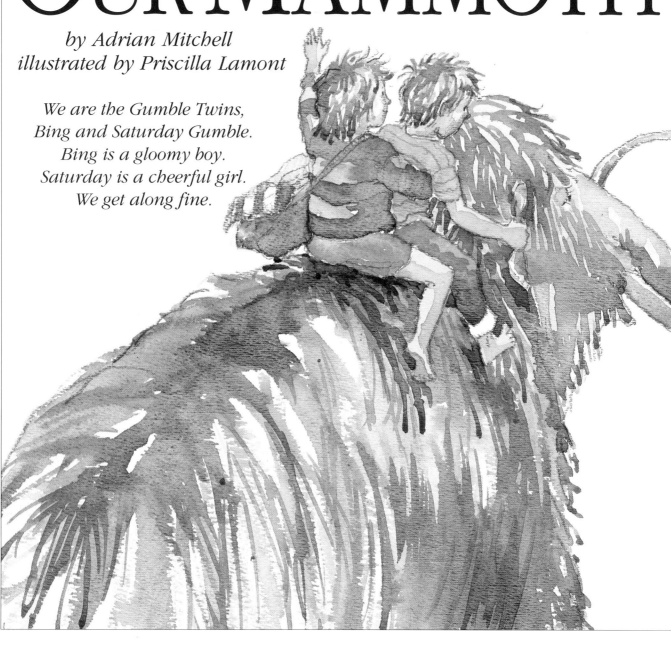

One day we took a bus to the beach. There was nobody else on the sand.

"The wind's too wild," said Bing.

"The water looks warm," said Saturday. So in we went.

The sea was green and cool. The waves were tall and bumpy.

Suddenly a mountain stood up in the sea – a blue and silver mountain. A floating mountain of ice.

"It's an iceberg!" we shouted together.

It was our first iceberg. The waves bumped the iceberg onto the beach.

"It's too slippery to climb," said Bing, "we'll break our backbones."

"I'll race you to the top," said Saturday. So we climbed to the top of the slippy drippy iceberg and we looked down into the ice.

At first we wished we hadn't looked: we were as scared as skittles. Deep down in the ice we saw two eyes. Two big eyes, all brown and golden. Two eyes, gazing up at us. Our legs wanted to run away but our heads wanted to stay.

So we stayed and we stared.

The iceberg was melting faster and faster. Out of one end came two curving tusks.

Then Saturday said, "Look – an elephant's trunk."

"Can't be," said Bing. "It's too big and too hairy."

We were too excited to be scared any more. We blew on the iceberg to make the ice melt faster.

Soon all the ice had dripped into the sand. There stood something, big as a lorry.

"It looks like a hill," said Bing.

"A hill with hair instead of grass," said Saturday.

"A hairy hill," we said together, and we knew it was really a mammoth, our first mammoth.

Our mammoth shivered and shook itself like a dog after a swim.

We jumped and squeaked.

Our mammoth stopped shaking. It looked up at the sun. It raised its trunk, then it trumpeted happily.

Our mammoth's hair was reddish-brown. Our mammoth's hair was strong like string.

"Hello, Mammoth," we said.

It sniffed us with its trunk.

"It seems to like us,"
said Saturday.
"You never know," said Bing.
We climbed up the side of our
mammoth. We sat in the long,
soft hair on its back. We were
high up in the air.
Our mammoth made a deep
purring sound. Then it started to
walk over the sand. We steered our
mammoth by its ears to the field
where we live in a caravan.
We were so happy we sang
all the way –
"Here we come on our mammoth."
When cars hooted at us our
mammoth hooted back.
When the mammoth saw our mum,
Sally Gumble, it raised its trunk
and gave a joyful honk. The honk
made our mum jump.
"Bing and Saturday, what on
earth is that?"
"It's our mammoth," we said.
"We found it in an iceberg
on the beach."
"Your mammoth is not an *it*," said
Mum, "your mammoth is a she.
She was frozen into that iceberg
many years ago. She must be hungry.
What do mammoths eat?"

We didn't
know but our
mammoth
knew.
The field
was full of
buttercups.
Our mammoth
gave a snorty
noise. She picked
two hundred
buttercups with her
trunk. She popped
them in her mouth.
She munched them up
and gulped them down.
"Can we keep her?" we asked.
"Of course we can," said Mum,
"she's beautiful. What shall we call her?"
Bing said, "Sandie, because we found
her on the beach."
Saturday said, "Hilda, because she
looks like a hill."
But in the end we named her Buttercup.

Mum found a very old book
in a shop. It was called:

HOW TO LOOK AFTER YOUR MAMMOTH.

It told us how to make Buttercup Pie.
The three of us ate a little of the pie
but Buttercup ate a lot.

NOISY

by Shirley Hughes

Noisy noises!

Pan lids clashing,

Dog barking,

Plate smashing,

Telephone ringing,

Baby bawling,

Midnight cats

Cat-a-wauling,

Door slamming,

Aeroplane zooming,

Vacuum cleaner

Vroom-vroom-vrooming,

And if I dance and sing a tune,

Baby joins in with a saucepan and spoon.

Gentle noises…

Dry leaves swishing,

Falling rain

Splashing, splishing,

Rustling trees

Hardly stirring,

Lazy cat

Softly purring.

Story's over,

Bedtime's come,

Crooning baby

Sucks his thumb.

All quiet, not a peep,

Everyone is fast asleep.

Parrot Cat

by Nicola Bayley

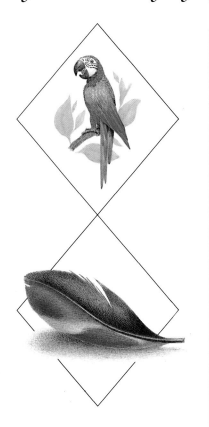

If I were a parrot
instead of a cat,

I would live
in the jungle,

I would fly
through the trees,

I would be coloured
so bright,

I would sit
on my nest,

I would talk
and squawk,

and if a snake
ever came,

I would quickly turn
back into a cat again.

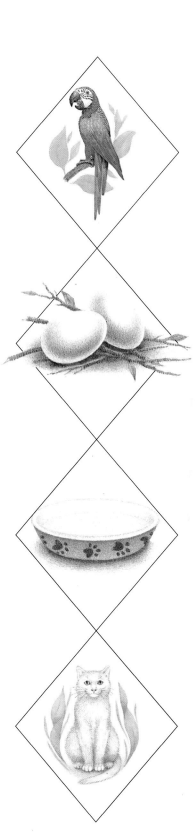

79

ROBERT

by Philippe

Robert lived with his mother and father in a big house. He had no brothers or sisters but he had lots of toys to play with. One day his mother came into his room. "Robert," she said, "be a little angel and run down to the shops for some biscuits. Aunt Susie is coming to tea."

On the way Robert met Mrs French. "Going shopping for your mummy?" she said. "What a good little boy you are."

At the flower stall the lady said, "That's Mrs Waters' little Robert. Isn't he a little darling?"

Mr Brown in the shop said, "Hello, little man. What can I do for you?"

"Little again!" Robert thought crossly. "Why do they all say I'm little?"

When Robert got home Aunt Susie was there.

"You little sweetie, my favourite biscuits!" she cooed. "Here, help yourself, my pet. I know what hungry tummies little boys like you always have."

"I am *not* little!" Robert screamed

I AM NOT LITTLE!!

THE GREAT

Dupasquier

furiously and he marched up to his room and slammed the door. From that moment on, Robert was a different boy. He was always staring into the mirror. "What rubbish," he'd say, "I'm not little. I'm *not*." He sulked. He did all kinds of silly things, trying to make himself look bigger.

Robert's behaviour got worse and worse. His parents were at their wits' end.

They tried everything. In the end they sent for the doctor. But that was no good. Robert bit him.

That night he dressed up as a horrible monster. "I'm a giant. I'm going to gobble you all up!" he shouted.

"This can't go on," said Mr Waters. "What the boy needs is a change."

So the next day they went on a trip to the zoo.

Robert was as horrid as ever. "I hate zoos," he said.

He hated the parrots; he hated the giraffes; he didn't even like the monkeys. Then a great big truck came into the zoo. On the truck was a cage and in the cage was an enormous tiger.

The keeper got up to check the bolts. "Keep back," he warned. "This fellow eats people for breakfast."

Just then a terrible thing happened. The tiger jumped at the cage door. The keeper fell over backwards. The door flew open.

The tiger leapt out. People were screaming and running everywhere. But Robert was left behind. He was standing in front of the cage. All by himself. Except for the tiger.

The tiger crouched, ready to spring. Someone screamed, "It's going to eat the little boy!"

But Robert had seen the open cage. The tiger pounced; Robert dashed inside. The tiger was right behind him. But before the tiger could reach him Robert squeezed out through the bars on the other side. No sooner had his feet touched the ground than he quickly ran round the truck. SLAM!

He had the cage door shut and bolted. The tiger was trapped.

The crowd couldn't believe it. Everyone cheered. Robert was a hero! They carried him round the zoo in triumph.

Next time he went shopping nobody called Robert little.

"My, what a big boy you are," Mrs French called as he passed.

"Stronger than a tiger," said the lady at the flower stall.

Everyone he met seemed to know about his great adventure.

"Here comes Robert the Great. Aren't we all proud of our big boy then?" said Aunt Susie the next time she came to tea.

"I'm not really big," Robert said, "or I couldn't have got through the bars of the cage, could I, Aunt Susie?"

TERRIBLE, TERRIBLE

There once was a terrible tiger, so terrible to see.
There once was a terrible tiger, as fierce as fierce can be.
There once was a terrible tiger that looked down from a tree.
There once was a terrible tiger that came creeping after me.
There once was a terrible tiger with teeth as sharp as sharp could be.
That terrible, terrible tiger – will he eat ME?
That terrible, terrible tiger, he roared … and leapt at me.

TIGER *by Colin and Jacqui Hawkins*

I cuddled that terrible tiger.
He's really my kitten, you see.

85

THE TOUGH PRINCESS

by Martin Waddell
illustrated by Patrick Benson

Once upon a time there lived a King and a Queen who weren't very good at it. They kept losing wars and mucking things up. They ended up living in a caravan parked beside a deep dark wood.

One day the Queen told the King that she was going to have a baby.

"Have a boy!" commanded the King. "He will grow up to be a hero, marry a rich princess and restore all of our fortunes!"

"Good idea!" said the Queen.

But when the baby came … it was a girl!

"Never mind," said the King. "She will grow up to be a beautiful princess. I will annoy a bad fairy and get the Princess into bother, and then a handsome prince will rescue her, and we'll all go off and live in his castle!"

"Good thinking!" said the Queen.

"We'll call her Rosamund."

"Ba!" said Rosamund.

The Princess grew up and up and up and up, until at last there wasn't room in the caravan to hold her. The King got a tent and pitched it outside.

"It's time you were married, Rosamund," the King told the Princess on her seventeenth birthday.

"Yes, Dad," said the Princess, "but…"

"I'll go off and arrange it," said the King.

The King went off into the deep dark wood to annoy some bad fairies.

The first fairy the King met was no use. She was a good one. She didn't even get angry when the King called her names.

The second fairy was bad, but she was only a beginner. She turned the King into a frog for making faces at her cat, but the spell wore off.

The third fairy was VERY bad. The King was awfully rude to her. "Aha!" cried the Bad Fairy.

"What do you love most in the world?"

"My daughter Rosamund!" cried the King hopefully.

"I will cast a spell on her!" cackled the Bad Fairy, who wasn't very bright, and she darted off to do it.

"Good-eee!" cried the King, because his get-the-princess-a-rich-prince plan was working.

The Bad Fairy came upon Princess Rosamund picking buttercups in a glade.

"Aha!" she cried.

"I am the Bad Fairy come to cast a spell on you.

Seven years shall you lie
Till a prince comes riding by…"
Biff! went Princess Rosamund, and she knocked the Bad Fairy out, bent her false teeth and bust up her glasses.
"You rotten, ungrateful thing, Rosamund!" said the Queen, picking up the Bad Fairy.
"I'll catch my prince my own way!" said Princess Rosamund.
The next day she borrowed the King's bike and rode off to seek her prince. Rosamund had a lot of adventures. She slew dragons and great worms and Nasty Knights. She rescued several princes who were quite rich, but she didn't like them, and so she threw them back. She did all the things a heroine ought to do, but she didn't catch her prince.

Princess Rosamund grew tired of rescuing princes and killing dragons, and her front wheel got buckled in a fight with a hundred-headed thing. In the end she set off sadly for home, carrying her bicycle.
"Hello, Mum. Hello, Dad. Hello, Bad Fairy," said Princess Rosamund when she got home.
"Where's your prince then?" said the King and the Queen and the Bad Fairy, who had moved in by this time.
"Haven't got one," said Princess Rosamund. "I'm not going to marry a ninny!"
"What about us!" cried the King and the Queen and the Bad Fairy.
"What are we supposed to live on if you can't come up with a prince?"
"That's your problem!" said Princess Rosamund. "I'm not going to…" and then she saw the sign.
"I'm doing this for me!" said Rosamund firmly, and she set off into the deep dark wood.
"You lot can look after yourselves!"
She bashed up several goblins and ghouls and the odd fairy (including several good ones by mistake), and finally she won through to the Enchanted Castle.
On a flower-strewn bed in the castle lay a beautiful prince.
Rosamund gave him a big smacky kiss.
The beautiful prince opened his eyes and took a look at Princess Rosamund.
"Cor! What a liberty!" he cried, and he biffed her one, right on her beautiful nose.
And Rosamund biffed him one right back!
It was love at first biff.
They biffed happily ever after.
The King and the Queen lived happily ever after too, and the Bad Fairy got even worse.

THIS WAY TO THE ENCHANTED PRINCE

TUMULT THE RABBIT

by David Lloyd
illustrated by Barbara Firth

Every day was a nice day for Tumult, until he first met Rosie Gilfillan. Nothing ever mattered, until he came out of a borrowed burrow that morning, and began going lippity-lop as easy as can be across a lovely summer meadow.

In a corner of the meadow Rosie Gilfillan was arguing with her boyfriend Horace. "Of course I like cabbage," she was saying. "It's just a stupid present to bring me, that's all."

"It's a champion cabbage," Horace said.

"You're a champion cabbage," Rosie said.

"Bless me!" said Horace, looking over Rosie's shoulder. "Look at that rabbit!" Rosie looked, Rosie saw, Rosie wanted.

"Look at its funny ears," she said, already imagining Tumult in a pie.

Everything about Tumult said "Take it easy, chuck! Let your ears hang down!" He was never in a hurry. He sauntered, he lolloped, he loped. There was always time to sit up and twitch the nose and whisker the whiskers.

He came to a hedge and went under it. He lolloped to the pond in the next meadow, and dipped his nose and drank.

He never saw Rosie coming after him with rabbit pie in mind. He never saw her slipping through the hedge, as cunning as a fox in her country ways.

He never saw Horace trudging after her, carrying the cabbage like a baby. Tumult wandered up the hill, with Rosie coming after him. Rosie was getting very close. There was a loud bellow in the hedge. It was Horace with the cabbage. Horace was badly caught in brambles. "Rosie!" he bellowed. "I'm stuck!" Tumult thumped and jumped and raced lippity-split away.

Rosie went face down in the grass. "Oh, Horace!" she said, as if everything were always his fault.

The second time Tumult and Rosie met was in the old woods, up on the hill. Tumult was lying by a fallen elm, just lazing around and dreaming. Everything about him said "Take it easy, chuck! Let your ears hang down!"

Rosie was in the woods looking for rabbits to put in pies. She saw Tumult, but he never saw her. Rosie was always so cunning. "Ah, you again," she thought with pleasure. "You with the funny ears!"

Rosie came creeping closer and closer. Cloud shadows moved across the clearing towards the fallen elm, and Rosie moved with them. Tumult lazed on, lost in his happy-go-lucky dream. Now Rosie was so close she could almost touch him. Rabbit pie was just one step away.

"Rosie!" someone bellowed. Tumult jumped and thumped and raced lippity-split away.

Rosie went down on her knees at the fallen elm like someone praying.

"Rosie!" someone shouted, coming through the trees. "I've brought you my champion marrow for a present." It was Horace.

"Champion marrow!" Rosie said, as if she were calling Horace names.

The third time Tumult met Rosie was in the warren by the stream. Tumult was having a go at digging a burrow, just to pass the time. His burrow was not very good, but this didn't matter, because Tumult always borrowed burrows anyway, when he wanted to go underground.

Rosie came into the warren. "Ah," she thought, spotting Tumult, "third time lucky maybe!"
Rosie crept closer.
Tumult scraped away at his burrow, which hardly looked like anything.
Rosie crept closer and closer.
Tumult rested for a moment. Everything about him said

"Take it easy, chuck! Let your ears hang down!" Rosie held her breath. No one made a sound. Rosie's hands went out like little rockets and caught Tumult round the middle.
Tumult couldn't go lippity-split. He couldn't go lippity-lop. He couldn't go lippity-anything.

He was well and truly caught. Rosie came out of the warren holding him very tight. She was smiling. Horace stepped out from a hiding place beside the path and bellowed.

"Stop, Rosie, stop!"

But it was too late. Rosie trod on a mat of ferns and the ground gave way beneath her. She fell into a pit with Tumult. There were vegetables on the floor. Horace peered over the edge of the pit.

"Rosie," he said.

Horace loved Rosie.

"I dug the pit to catch the rabbit," he said. "The vegetables were bait."

"Oh, Horace," Rosie said out of the pit.

"It was going to be a present," Horace said. Now Horace had to rescue Rosie. But first Rosie had to pass him Tumult.

Horace held Tumult gently for a moment, looking at his funny, hang-down ears. Then he put him on the ground to have both hands free for Rosie.

"Horace!" Rosie cried out. Tumult thumped and jumped and raced lippity-split away. He was in a most amazing hurry. Everything about him said "Go, chuck, go! Button your ears and beat it!"

There are seven animals in the gang today. They have all had great escapes. They live together and travel together. They are friends. Today they are all in a cave by the sea, and it is Tumult's turn to tell the story.

"Every day was always a nice day," he begins, "until I first met Rosie Gilfillan."

And the story which he tells is the story you just heard.

THE WALKER BEAR'S BOOKSHELF

The stories and pictures in *The Walker Bear* were taken from 35 favourite picture books. The original version of each book had more pictures or more poems or more stories, and sometimes it was one of a series of books about the same characters. Here are some details about the books, and a list of other books by the same authors and illustrators.

8 **Tom and Pippo Read a Story**
Helen Oxenbury
From the Pippo series. The other books are Tom and Pippo Make a Mess; Tom and Pippo Go for a Walk; Tom and Pippo and the Washing Machine; Tom and Pippo Go Shopping; Tom and Pippo's Day; Tom and Pippo in the Garden; Tom and Pippo See the Moon; Tom and Pippo and the Dog; Tom and Pippo in the Snow; Tom and Pippo Make a Friend; Pippo Gets Lost.

10 **They Came from Aargh!**
Russell Hoban/Colin McNaughton
From The Hungry Three series. The other books are The Great Fruit Gum Robbery; The Flight of Bembel Rudzuk; The Battle of Zormla.

14 **This Is the Bear**
Sarah Hayes/Helen Craig
Other books by Hayes/Craig are This Is the Bear and the Picnic Lunch; Crumbling Castle; Mary, Mary. Other books illustrated by Helen Craig include The Yellow House by Blake Morrison, and the Susie and Alfred series, which she wrote herself.

16 **Just Like Archie**
Niki Daly
From the Storytime series. The other books are Teddy's Ear; Look at Me!; Ben's Gingerbread Man; Monsters Are Like That; Thank You Henrietta.

18 **All Fall Down**
Helen Oxenbury
From the Helen Oxenbury Big Board Books series. The other books are Tickle, Tickle; Clap Hands; Say Goodnight.

20 **Bad Egg**
Sarah Hayes/Charlotte Voake
Other books illustrated by Charlotte Voake include Over the Moon (a nursery rhyme collection); First Things First (a baby's companion); Tom's Cat and Mrs Goose's Baby, which she also wrote; Duck and The Ridiculous Story of Gammer Gurton's Needle, both by David Lloyd; Amy Said by Martin Waddell; The Best of Aesop's Fables, retold by Margaret Clark.

22 **Tales from Baron Munchausen**
Adrian Mitchell/Patrick Benson
An excerpt from The Baron Rides Out, from The Adventures of Baron Munchausen series. The other books are The Baron on the Island of Cheese and The Baron All at Sea.

24 **Cat and Dog**
David Lloyd/Clive Scruton
Other books illustrated by Clive Scruton include Four Black Puppies by Sally Grindley; Sidney the Monster by David Wood; Our Sleepysaurus (a Read Aloud) by Martin Waddell; Wompus Galumpus by Gina Wilson; Tottie Pig's Special Birthday and Tottie Pig's Noisy Christmas, both by Vivian French.

26 **Charlie Meadows**
Russell Hoban/Martin Baynton

An excerpt from Ponders, a Read Aloud containing eight stories. Other Read Alouds include Andrew McAndrew by Bernard Mac Laverty, illustrated by Duncan Smith; Private Nose by John Robert Taylor, illustrated by Emanuel Schongut; Hazel the Guinea-Pig by A.N. Wilson, illustrated by Jonathan Heale.

28 **Where's Wally?**
Martin Handford
Part of one of 12 scenes in Where's Wally? The other Wally books are Where's Wally Now?; Where's Wally? 3 The Fantastic Journey; Where's Wally? The Ultimate Fun Book!

30 **Till Owlyglass**
Michael Rosen/Fritz Wegner

An excerpt from The Wicked Tricks of Till Owlyglass. Other books by Michael Rosen include We're Going on a Bear Hunt, illustrated by Helen Oxenbury; The Horribles, illustrated by John Watson; Little Rabbit Foo Foo, illustrated by Arthur Robins. Fritz Wegner also illustrated The Sneeze by David Lloyd.

32 **Tell Us a Story**
Allan Ahlberg/Colin McNaughton
A Blue Book from the 16-book series Red Nose Readers – a library of hilarious words and pictures to encourage all early readers.

34 **Dad's Back**
Jan Ormerod
From the series Baby Books. The other books are Reading; Sleeping; Messy Baby. Jan Ormerod also illustrated the series Little Ones; the series New Baby Books; The Story of Chicken Licken; Eat Up, Gemma and Happy Christmas, Gemma, both by Sarah Hayes; Kitten Day; The Frog Prince; When We Went to the Zoo.

36 **Ten in the Bed**
Penny Dale
Other books by Penny Dale are Bet You Can't!; Wake Up, Mr. B!; Once There Were Giants and Rosie's Babies, both by Martin Waddell; The Stopwatch by David Lloyd.

38 **Can't You Sleep, Little Bear?**
Martin Waddell/Barbara Firth

Other books by Waddell/Firth are The Park in the Dark and We Love Them. Other books illustrated by Barbara Firth include "Quack!" said the billy-goat by Charles Causley; The Munros'